JONNY ZUCKER began his career in radio and is now a writer
and primary school teacher. Along the way he has played in
several bands and has worked as a stand-up comedian. Jonny has
written two books for adults: *A Class Act* and *Dream Decoder*.
He lives in London with his wife and their young son.

JAN BARGER COHEN, originally from Arkansas in the U.S.A.,
is a well-established illustrator of children's books.
Her previous titles include *Bible Stories for the Very Young*,
the Little Animals series, *Incy Wincy Moo-Cow*, *Who Can Fly?*,
Who Can Jump?, *Who Eats This?* and *Who Lives Here?*.
She lives in East Sussex with her husband
and a cocker spaniel called Tosca.

For Mum, Dad, Naomi and Albert – J.Z.
To Geoffrey and Audrey – J.B.C.

First published in Great Britain in 2003 by
Frances Lincoln Limited, 4 Torriano Mews,
Torriano Avenue, London NW5 2RZ

www.franceslincoln.com

First paperback edition 2004

British Library Cataloguing in Publication Data available on request

ISBN 0-7112-2019-0

Printed in Singapore

1 3 5 7 9 8 6 4 2

The Publishers would like to thank Bryan Reuben for checking the text and illustrations.

FESTIVAL TIME!

It's Party Time!

A Purim Story

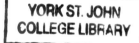
Jonny Zucker

Illustrated by Jan Barger Cohen

FRANCES LINCOLN

It's Purim, so Mum and Dad tell us the story of good Queen Esther and wicked Haman.

We take a gift basket
of food to our
friends' house.

I make a special Purim mask
and we all wear fancy dress.

We go to a friend's house and play party games.

Everyone eats Hamantaschen.
I love the sweet seeds
on top.

We give money to charity for those who are not as lucky as we are.

We go to synagogue.
When we hear Haman's name
we boo and shake our rattles.
We're so happy our people
were saved!

What is Purim about?

Purim is a celebration of the story of Queen Esther and how she saved the Jews from certain death at the hands of Haman.

About 2500 years ago, King Ahasuerus ruled the great Persian Empire. He held a beauty contest to find a queen, and the winner was Esther, the niece of a Jew called Mordecai, but Esther did not tell the king that she was Jewish. One day, Mordecai overheard two men plotting to kill the king. He told Esther, who then told the king what Mordecai had overheard, and the plotters were executed.

The king had a very powerful adviser called Haman. Haman demanded that everyone should kneel to him, but Mordecai refused, saying that Jews kneel only to God. Haman was angry and wanted to kill all the Jews. He told the king that the Jews were conspiring against him, and the king agreed to let Haman kill them. Mordecai heard the proclamation and told Esther what Haman was planning. So Esther invited the king and Haman to a dinner party. The king was so pleased, he offered Esther any gift she wished. She said, "I'll tell you tomorrow night."

That night, the king could not sleep. He was reminded of how Mordecai saved him and realised he had not rewarded Mordecai. The king asked Haman how he should reward a man he wanted to honour. Haman thought the king was talking about him and said that he should be dressed in the king's robe and led through the city on the king's horse by a nobleman calling out, "This is the man the king delights to honour." "Good," said the king. "Go and honour Mordecai." This made Haman even angrier towards the Jews.

At Esther's second dinner party, she told the king, "I am to be killed along with my people. I ask you to spare us." "Who gave such an order?" asked the king, horrified because he still did not realise that Esther was Jewish. Esther pointed to Haman. So Haman was executed instead of the Jews and Mordecai became the king's adviser.

Today, Purim is celebrated with parties and costumes. **Hamantaschen** are eaten which are made in the shape of Haman's three-cornered hat. It is customary to give gifts of two or more kinds of food (**mishloach manot**) to friends and to give **Tzedakah** (charity). The story of Esther is read from a scroll called the **Megillah**. Everyone makes a noise to blot out the name of Haman.

MORE TITLES IN THE FESTIVAL TIME! SERIES BY JONNY ZUCKER AND JAN BARGER COHEN

Apples and Honey – A Rosh Hashanah Story
See how a Jewish family celebrates
New Year with this delightful book!

ISBN 0-7112-2016-6 PB

Eight Candles to Light – A Chanukah Story
Follow a family as they light the menorah,
open presents and eat latkes.

ISBN 0-7112-2017-4 PB

Four Special Questions! – A Passover Story
Read about matzah, the Seder plate, the four
questions and the hunt for the Afikoman.

ISBN 0-7112-2018-2 PB

Frances Lincoln titles are available from all good bookshops.
You can also buy books and find out more about your favourite titles,
authors and illustrators at our website: www.franceslincoln.com.